Fun-to-Read Picture Books have been grouped into three approximate readability levels by Bernice and Cliff Moon. Yellow books are suitable for beginners; red books for readers acquiring first fluency; blue books for more advanced readers.

This book has been assessed as Stage 6 according to *Individualised Reading*, by Bernice and Cliff Moon, published by The Centre for the Teaching of Reading, University of Reading School of Education.

First published 1987 by
Walker Books Ltd
184-192 Drummond Street
London NW1 3HP

First printed 1987
Printed and bound by
L.E.G.O., Vicenza, Italy

British Library Cataloguing in Publication Data
West, Colin
"Hello, great big bullfrog!" (Fun-to-Read
picture books)
I. Title II. Series
823'.914[J] PZ7

ISBN 0-7445-0561-5

# "Hello, great big bullfrog!"

Written and illustrated by
## Colin West

WALKER BOOKS
LONDON

"Hello, I'm a great big bullfrog," said the great big bullfrog.

"Hello, great big bullfrog! Guess who I am!"

"I'm a great big rat,"
said the great big rat
to the great big bullfrog.

"Hello, great big rat!
Guess who I am!"

"I'm a great big wart-hog,"
said the great big wart-hog
to the great big rat
and the great big bullfrog.

"Hello, great big wart-hog!
Guess who I am!"

"I'm a great big tiger,"
said the great big tiger
to the great big wart-hog
and the great big rat
and the great big bullfrog.

"Hello, great big tiger! Guess who I am!"

"I'm a great big bear,"
said the great big bear
to the great big tiger
and the great big wart-hog
and the great big rat
and the great big bullfrog...

"Let's have a great big HULLABALOO!"

But the great big bullfrog
didn't want a great big hullabaloo.

He didn't feel so great and big any more. He felt a tiddly little bullfrog.

"Goodbye, everybody!"
said the not so great big bullfrog.

But suddenly...

"Hello, great
big bullfrog!
Guess who I am!"

"I'm a great big bumble-bee,"
said the great big bumble-bee.

"And I'm a great big bullfrog!"
said the great big bullfrog.
"A great
   great
      great big bullfrog!"